Let's Stick Together!

A GOLDEN BOOK • NEW YORK

ISBN 978-0-7364-3354-9
randomhousekids.com
MANUFACTURED IN CHINA
10 9 8 7 6 5 4 3 2 1

Elsa uses her magical ice powers to create
a winter wonderland inside the castle!

One of Elsa's magic ice blasts hits Anna by mistake.
It makes Anna very cold!

The king and queen rush the girls to the trolls.
They hope the trolls' magic can help them!

The trolls help Anna, but Elsa is forced to wear gloves to keep everyone safe from her ice powers.

Anna is lonely without her sister.

Many years later, a grown-up Elsa prepares
to become Queen of Arendelle.

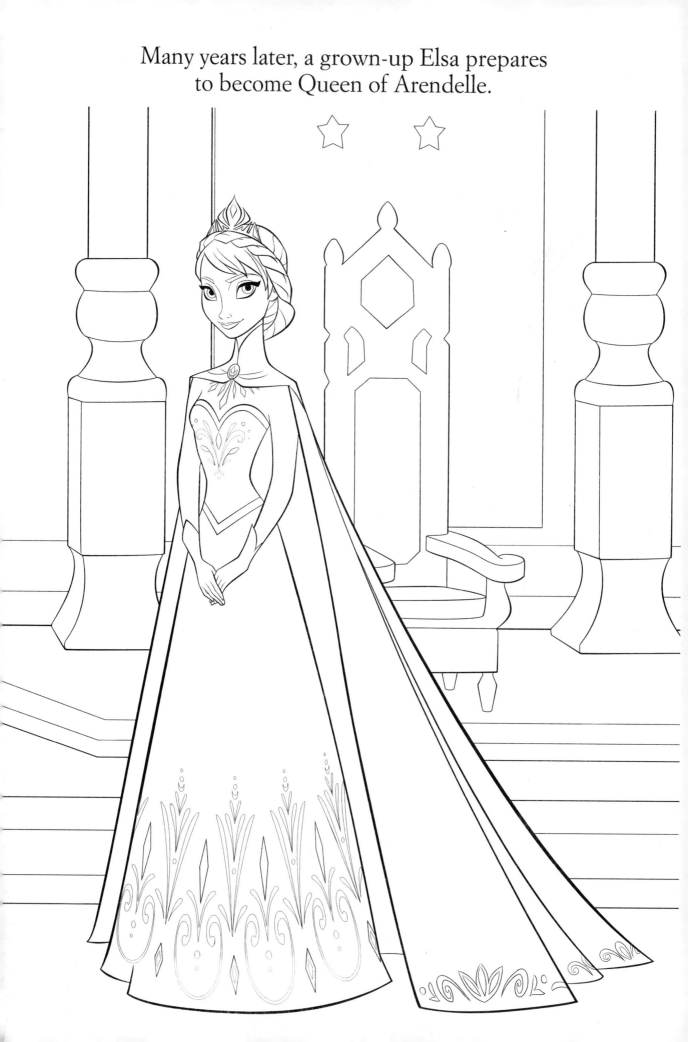

Kristoff is an ice harvester. He lives in the mountains.
He sells ice to the people of Arendelle.

Anna is excited! Lots of people arrive
in Arendelle for the ceremony.

Elsa is scared. She tries to control her ice power, but without her gloves, she freezes everything she touches!

Anna is excited for the coronation,
but Elsa can't wait for it to be over.

Anna is proud of her sister!

Anna shares a dance with Prince Hans.

After an argument with Anna,
Elsa loses control of her magical ice powers!

Everyone is shocked by Elsa's ice power!

Elsa runs away from Arendelle!

Elsa builds a magnificent ice palace on the North Mountain.

Anna must find her sister!

Anna meets Kristoff while buying supplies.

Kristoff and his reindeer, Sven, help Anna search for Elsa.

Uh-oh—wolves!

The wolf chase ends with a terrible crash!
Anna and Sven pull Kristoff to safety.

Anna meets Olaf!

Olaf dreams of sunny summer days.

Olaf and Sven become good friends.

Anna is determined to reach Elsa.
Olaf knows how to find her!

Elsa is the Snow Queen.

Anna asks Elsa to come home with her.

Elsa is afraid to leave her ice palace.

Elsa accidentally hits Anna with an icy blast!

Elsa creates Marshmallow to scare Anna
and her friends off the mountain.

Marshmallow chases Anna and Kristoff to the mountain's edge.

Kristoff helps Anna climb down the mountain.

Oh, no! Anna's hair is turning white because of Elsa's icy blast!

Elsa worries about what she has done.

Kristoff takes Anna to see the magical trolls.

An old troll tells Anna that only an
act of true love can save her.

Kristoff tries to save Anna.

Hans captures Elsa.

Anna thinks a kiss from Hans will save her.
But he doesn't really love her.

Anna is trapped!

Elsa breaks free.

Sven wants Kristoff to go back to Anna.

Olaf helps Anna escape!

Anna is turning to ice!

Elsa thinks it's too late to save Anna.

Kristoff tries to save Anna.

Anna

I'm an expert in the Snow

MY SISTER · MY HERO

Olaf

Elsa

Anna

Elsa

Anno

Olaf

Sparkling elegant Ice

Ice Crystals

Follow your heart

I Love Warm Hugs

MY SISTER · MY HERO

Winter Magic

Follow your Heart

Sister Queens

Follow your Heart

Graceful & gorgeous

Sisters Forever

Spiralling Snow

Forever Sisters

Winter Wishes

Eternal Winter

I Love Warm Hugs

WARM HUGS

Sisters Forever

Anna saves Elsa's life. But then she is frozen.

Anna is saved by her love for Elsa!

Anna and Elsa learn to work together.

Elsa helps Olaf enjoy warmer weather.

Elsa makes a winter wonderland.

Anna thanks Kristoff for helping to save her sister.

Finally, Anna and Elsa can play together again!
Elsa makes another winter wonderland in the Great Hall.

Anna and Elsa are friends again.
Nothing will keep these sisters apart!

Anna and Elsa enjoy spending time together.

Olfa joins Anna and Elsa as they play in the mountains.

Elsa and Anna have a friendly snowball fight!

On their way back to the castle, the sisters
see a young reindeer trapped on a ledge.

Together Anna, Elsa, and Olaf help their new friend to safety.

Olaf, Elsa, and Anna love their new reindeer friend!

Elsa uses her icy powers to speed them back to the castle.

Anna and Elsa are happy to be
back home with their new friend.